THIS CITY BREATHING

THIS CITY BREATHING

CHAD DEAN

Thera Books
Sacramento, California
SAY / SOMETHING

for Pema and Jenn

"[I don't want to make] destruction into a beautiful experience. I think of it as part of an immensely wasteful condition." —Gordon Matta-Clark

BOOK 1 PART 1

HOW TO SPEND A DAY INSIDE.

1
WHAT DOES ALLEN SEE
WHEN HE OPENS HIS EYES?

The alabaster ceiling. Blinking, wider and wider each time, he takes in the fixed rotation of five ceiling fan blades, constructed of pressboard, freshly coated cream trimmed in beige ornamental lattice. Spinning steady through the fading gray. To the right, on Allen's nightstand, is his alarm clock. Vanilla-cased red lights against the black backdrop so the time is clearly visible. But Allen already knows it is 7:45. This is the time he gets up every weekday morning. This is a good thing.

His bed is in pretty decent shape.

Allen feels okay. The new comforter he ordered that promised to regulate body temperature and prevent him from waking up saturated from sweat seems to be working. His new sheets, the highest thread count his budget would allow—480—feel better against his skin than the ones they replaced. It seems he got an acceptable night of sleep.

Bedroom is nice. In order.

This room is an almost perfect cube. Newly painted Snowbound, a color released two months ago. Allen's Robert Ryman is still hanging on the wall opposite the bed, beyond his toes pointed upward. It is the last thing he saw before lying down. Everything is the way he likes it.

2
WHAT DOES ALLEN HEAR?

The voices of men. Talk about the days. The day to come and the day just past. Allen is committed to listening as much as he can. It is important to know how things had gone, how they were going. Even if they aren't going so well.

The air condition is working. He can hear it humming if he makes a point to listen for the sound. The exact amount of noise confirms that it is pushing out the proper amount of air at the determined temperature.

If it's functioning properly, Allen can hear slightly the murmurs of Baltimore outside, but nothing too clearly. He likes to know the city is there, but he doesn't want to find himself knowing more about his neighbors than he should.

It is also important to mind your own business.

3
WHAT DOES ALLEN DO EVERY DAY BEFORE HE GETS OUT OF BED?

Breathe.

He fills his belly, to the count of eight, with slow deep breaths. Releases them with the same cadence. Visualizes a public garden in Holland, a picture frame of yellow tulips offset by a single red flower in the corner, for six breath cycles.

Taking in the air in his own room, in his own house, to fill all his insides.

This helps his mind reach a place of relaxation.

Through these steps Allen can be ready for the day.

He learned how to do so from an electronic newsletter for which he did not register.

4
WHAT WILL ALLEN DO TODAY?

Stay inside.

It's better in here.

Another full day ahead. Time to get out of bed. Time to get dressed and leave the bedroom.

Allen has more space. A living/dining/television/sitting/working room, full of furniture. Kitchen table, recliner, television stand and television, computer station and computer.

The best thing is his cream-colored leather easy chair. So comfortable and it has a sleeve draped over one of the arms that was made to hold remote controls and magazines. Allen uses it to hold his newspaper.

He needs today's paper now.

It's on the porch.

Allen moves toward the glass circle on his front door and looks through. He is looking for his neighbor—or anyone else who might be on his street. There is no one there, but still he waits, until his next-door neighbor, the woman on the other side of the wall, has gotten herself and her rusting red grocery cart down the marble steps.

When he can no longer hear or see her, Allen counts to 60 five times.

This is how long it takes for her to disappear.

Allen does not want to look like a crazy person.

When he is sure she is gone he unlocks the deadbolt, cracks his door a little more than the width of his skull, and slides his head through the slice of space now open.

It smells like springtime a little, from the trees recently planted by a couple with two newish kids four doors down who moved in after the first child was born but before the second. The scent of their blooms mingled with the odor of fried dough and batter from the diner two blocks away. Allen has never been, but read about it once.

He can feel them both, trees and bread, inside his nostrils.

The thing he needs is near the center of his porch, but he cannot reach it, so Allen retreats. He takes a wooden-handled, green-topped rake resting against the door molding and looks through his peephole. No one is coming. He moves left of frame, reproduces the crack, and rakes in *The Baltimore Sun*.

Allen holds the paper and feels the warm, familiar satisfaction of accomplishment.

He has been using the same rake for thirteen years.

This is how long he has been indoors.

But it's not like he meant for it to happen.

Now it's time for breakfast. Allen will have rye toast and oatmeal with two pinches of sugar. Always after gathering the news, always before reading.

Near silence is what Allen takes with his breakfast. Only the sound of his crunching teeth and metal spoon scraping empty his oatmeal bowl. He eats and listens to his mouth while unbuttered flecks of bread decorate the ceramic plate Allen is careful to eat over. He collects with a cloth napkin whatever stray crumbs hit the table so that when breakfast is finished it will appear that no meal was ever eaten at the table.

After breakfast, on the good days, Allen uses the bathroom. Today is a good day.

His belly now full, his system now flushed, Allen can concentrate on the paper. He does not read the Front Page, Sports, or the Business section. Allen prefers In Lifestyle. On Monday through Wednesday, he will do the crossword puzzle but today is Friday so he will do the word jumble. Today the word is INCLUSIVE. It has been jumbled to CUSLNIEVI.

In Lifestyle Allen reads fashion and entertainment. There is a picture of a casually dressed world-famous movie star, positioning herself and several bags into a midsized luxury crossover SUV. A new television show about emergency workers in a city Allen went to once will debut next Tuesday night. He already has a show he watches then.

Regulating screen time is essential. If Allen spends too much time in front of the TV, or staring at his phone, he gets grumpy. He is mindful to sit with the paper until 11 in the morning, when it is game show time.

The Price Is Right is the best. It's fun to try to guess the price of things; his favorite is trying to decide which item is worth more. Today Allen tries to determine the relative values of a dinnerware hutch and a set of cobalt-blue mountain bikes. He thinks the hutch is worth more. Allen is right.

After the game show Allen goes right into stories— that's what his mom would call them—every weekday from 12 until three. He has a different routine for the weekends.

Starting at 12, ending at one, Allen is focused on a wealthy patriarch's trial for a murder he probably did not commit. He has been set up by some members of his family while some others are trying to save him. Today is cliffhanger day. In the end the old man is escorted from the courtroom. Some people in the gallery smile, and some sulk. Everyone has a plan for Monday.

At 1 a young couple with a newly pregnant wife are trapped in a crumbling waterfront warehouse. They've been there since Wednesday, when the wife's jilted lover tricked them into entering. Help is on the way. At 1:57 part of the room collapses.

Next, Allen mostly hears people arguing about

money and maybe children's custody. They all live in a big house with a lot of antiques, but this is the time Allen will take his nap, so he is generally confused about the two to three story line.

5
WHAT WILL ALLEN DO TONIGHT?

Make sure he is ready for the morning.

At 5pm Allen hears the daily alarm he has set so that he doesn't nap for too long and wakes up to the evening news. It is never good, really, but is exceptionally bad at this moment. The city is on fire, and no one likes the police. Or some people like them very much, but the people setting fires do not like them at all.

Allen is hungry. It is time to make dinner.

Out of a thin wooden cabinet found online, converted to a kitchen pantry, six feet tall, the same height as Allen, he removes penne pasta, Greek olive oil, and his two remaining cloves of garlic. It's fine as long as he remembers to order more tomorrow. After the water has come to a boil, after the pasta has been cooking for two minutes, Allen heats two tablespoons of oil in a pan and continually repositions the pressed garlic for 45 seconds before removing it from the gas flame. Pasta, oil, garlic, salt, and pepper are combined in a large glass bowl before being transferred to plate and topped with parmesan cheese from a green cylinder that always clumps together in the refrigerator so Allen has to really shake it to get the right amount to come out. For a little while he ate directly from the mixing bowl but decided that was too uncivilized. A dinner plate adds structure.

It is important to go slow and appreciate what you are doing, even the smallest task, even the things that seem so meaningless, but Allen cannot help but rush a little through the dinner cleanup. He cannot help but anticipate.

He shouldn't hurry either though. Allen knows he needs to slow down.

Tomorrow he will do yoga for 20 minutes, a program designed for men over 60, people Allen's age, to maximize movement and longevity, so he lays out a pair of yoga pants that cost him $98 and a t-shirt that cost him $50 but could be the last t-shirt he ever has to buy according to the ad.

In the shower Allen collects himself and gets ready. His body is as strong now as it ever was, maybe stronger from 11 years of yoga. He isn't losing any hair; he's got his grandfather's hair, as thick as when he was 35 or 50. Of course it's completely white. His lungs feel strong, and even though he doesn't have any older pictures of himself to compare to, his eyes, in the foggy bathroom mirror, don't seem any less blue.

His heart rate is increasing, and he knows by exactly how much. But it's not anything he needs to call a doctor about. Allen is just getting excited.

6
WHAT IS THE BEST PART OF THE DAY?

The after-dinner ritual.

Everything Allen needs now is waiting for him at the workstation. It used to be more complicated. At first, he had to buy a video camera and a tripod, then find a place in his house to keep it, out of the way. He used to have to set the whole thing up every night. The tripod first, then the camera, then himself in front of it all. Now he just needs to sit down and turn on the camera inside his phone. It's a very intuitive, expensive phone, easy for him to operate.

Now with words Allen remembers the day. To appreciate all that was achieved and earned. Radio voices, his meditative breathing, breakfast, TV and napping, his dinner, and now this too. He thinks about the hutch and how it might look in the eating area of the woman who could have won it. Today she did not. He thinks about the man going to jail who will most likely be released, if not next Monday then a Monday soon after. The couple in the falling down place. Will the baby survive the roof collapse? The adults will, most likely. They are part of the core cast, and Allen has read nothing about either actor leaving the show. But the baby is not a staple. Survival cannot be assured. Allen doesn't have much to say about whatever is happening with the money in the last one. His nap was pleasant, his dinner was essential, easy, and he is so happy to be at this station, making record of his day through video and writing.

Allen always gives himself this one hour.

It was the recommendation of a person, from when Allen lived with people.

To help with memory and keep him from getting too bored.

Allen has 13 years of tapes, arranged chronologically in a closet. Obnoxious black VHS cassettes, then CDs he would burn, now sticks of memory.

When he is sure everything is properly backed up and secure, he can watch a little more TV. Since it's Friday, Allen will watch a show about a female psychic who teams up with an eccentric male detective who doesn't get along with anyone but through the help of his partner is able to solve a mystery by the end of each episode. Every Friday Allen thinks this is his favorite night to watch television.

10:15 is bedtime, but he won't fall asleep until 11. He checks his phone one last time. Allen was expecting a delivery today. It's okay it didn't come. It will be here tomorrow. He is sure. Sliding under the covers, careful not to disturb the bedding too much, Allen remembers to breathe and smile and focus on the circling pressboard blades until he is no longer conscious.

BOOK 1 PART 2

A WINDOW IS BROKEN AGAIN.

7
WHAT FUCKING NOW?

Something is wrong. It's 1:37 in the morning. He shouldn't be awake, but the noise he thought was part of his dream at first is part of the real world, right outside and loud enough to wake him. Allen is also, now that he thinks about it, covered in glass.

It came from his window. It *is* his window.

Directly above him is not the ceiling fan blades but what looks like a metal giraffe's head, like the ones you can feed at the Baltimore Zoo that he read about last week. It's a streetlamp. Allen doesn't really care though. His first concern is his skin being cut by window glass. Any tiny shard could scrape against part of him, drawing blood. Blood would stain his new sheets.

The metal is sliding against wooden window frame. He can hear it shaking more glass loose before rising up and disappearing from his room.

"Jesus fucking Christ be careful."

"Fuck off. It's goddamn…"

That's all he hears of the voices. Metal clanks against metal, a car moves away, and Allen is alone.

But what kind of alone, Allen cannot say. He lies petrified. Motionless. Makes himself stiff. Unsure if he has been compromised by the uncountable fragments spread all over him and his bedroom. He has an itch on his leg that is probably not glass. It cannot be glass because his comforter is too thick to be penetrated. A benefit of buying such heavy down.

Clear what he needs to do next: get out of bed (being careful not to slice open his foot on any floor shards) and clean up this mess; only, Allen isn't moving. He cannot bring his hands out from under the safety of the goose feather duvet.

Breathe. Breathe the way you have been instructed, Allen tells himself, but it's impossible to fill his stomach without raising the blanket, getting more shit everywhere, putting more in his way. Unable to properly collect the oxygen needed, he mentally records the times and causes of previous window fractures. This is the fifth time.

It is the first at night.

It is not okay for Allen to be alone with a broken window at night.

Anyone can come in.

This city is not safe.

Everyone says so.

In the all the news and on the television.

He has to do something.

It won't take too long. He can handle this. First assess the damage.

Allen lies as still and breathes as deeply as possible until 2:05. He tries to imagine doing the next necessary thing.

It won't be hard. Years of yoga have given Allen exceptional control over his body and mind. By many metrics he is in the best shape of his life. Even at 63. Picturing his body like a smooth, flexible board, Allen slides away from the window, toward the bedroom door where he can reach the light switch and where hopefully there is less danger of being sliced. He should have ordered the ceiling fan with the remote-control light. Maybe he'll do that next week.

A pretty big fucking mess, he can see that now. But he is up to the task. Clean up tonight, call to have the window repaired tomorrow. Same as the other times, almost.

For 20 minutes Allen collects broken glass and puts his bedroom back in order. He has learned to keep replacements for his most essential items—robes, slippers, bedding and curtains—stockpiled in his house in case something like this happens.

Storage is on the second floor, which Allen never visits, or remembers he has, unless he needs to replace something.

Obviously, he doesn't have an extra bedroom window. He wouldn't know how to install a thing like that anyway. A thick black trash bag, heavy duty, designed to collect yard debris, will make for an acceptable hole cover until tomorrow, when he will pay someone whatever it takes for a same-day repair.

When everything is back to normal, as much as possible, a sleepy Allen returns to bed. Not in bed but on it. He did a good job, and even if the new barricade is not secure enough, not secure at all, there is nothing he can do about it. If someone is going to come in to rob or murder him, he will have to accept that as his fate since he has done all he can to protect himself.

He should just get under the covers because sitting on the edge, staring at the billowing window bag, isn't helping. It makes a lot of noise snapping around with the wind outside. No matter how much tape applied, Baltimore air leaks through. The bedroom temperature is all wrong.

He doesn't lie down though; he can't or won't pretend like everything is normal. It's not as easy as he thought it would be to accept his impending demise.

Christ, will he be able to get any sleep at all? Will he have to stay awake, on guard till morning? Is that the only way he can be sure he'll make it through the night alive?

Impossible in the moment to know, so he continues to sit on the side of his bed staring at the trash bag, looking at the floor around his feet for glass, thinking about the different ways he might be found dead and about how much of the wrong kind of air is getting inside his room and body every second.

8
IS IT MORNING?

It's light out, but not the right kind of light. The time is 9:57. There is a commercial on the radio. Allen must have fallen asleep sideways on top of his covers. The thick plastic bag is keeping out more sun than his undyed canvas curtains ever could, like the black-out shades he installed six years ago that made it too hard for him to get up in the morning. It might be half as bright as it was yesterday.

Allen hears voices, but they are the wrong kind too. They come from outside.

Someone is running to the store, needs to hold five dollars.

Someone else, who doesn't care what that asshole does, isn't going anywhere.

And another someone else can go fuck themselves.

Allen doesn't want to listen to any of this. He's not nosey. Other people's problems are their own.

Trucks from the post office around the corner are moving up and down the street; they have a specific kind of sound, old metal lurching up the hill carrying new cardboard boxes. There is a dog that is most likely part beagle; it sounds like the one Allen had as a child, always barking in the morning. Usually muffled. Now everything is closer than it should be. Allen overslept. Today is already going poorly.

He didn't get enough rest and what he did get wasn't good enough. A lot needs to be done today. Just because it's Saturday doesn't mean Allen has nothing to do.

Too bad he doesn't feel like doing any of it now. He shouldn't have to worry about this.

Jerking the robe down from its hook, shoving his feet into their slippers, Allen grumbles his way into the easy chair.

First of all he's hungry. Behind schedule. Normally he would have already eaten by now. Allen doesn't want to think about how much of the day he already wasted lying in bed staring at the window and listening to the things happening outside. He looks like shit, can see that in the curved black TV reflection, didn't even tie his bathrobe so the left half of his torso and his left leg are completely exposed. This is no way to spend a day. He needs to get his shit together. Or at least take a nap and get a fresh start when he is in a better mood. He can't let this inconvenience ruin his whole day. Even if it is a pretty big deal and totally unfair.

9
CAN ALLEN GET HIS SHIT TOGETHER?

Yes, for sure he can. He needs to center himself and draw plenty of clean deep breaths, as many as he needs, take stock of his day, assess what he is capable of, which is still quite a lot if he's being honest with himself, and make the most of a bad situation.

He should eat first. Maybe then take a nap because at least that way he won't wake up so hungry.

Breakfast sucks though. It's waffles on Saturday, and normally Allen really likes these. They're kind of an end-of-the-week reward for him with the grass-fed butter and tablespoon of maple syrup, but he doesn't enjoy them like he should, and he's not sitting properly, slumped over the table and only thinking about how his window needs to be fixed, and he doesn't want to have to do that today.

10
WHAT CAN ALLEN REASONABLY EXPECT OF HIMSELF?

At the very least he can get organized mentally by making a list of the things that would need to be done on a regular Saturday, and then he can have a visual sense of how the extra things he has to do can be added to his daily agenda while allowing for the time he lost when he didn't get out of bed correctly.

Without order, this life is not easy.

New window was not planned; something will have to be cut out to make room. A list will help. Some parts of his day are pure luxury. Allen can deprive himself of something superfluous and get back on schedule.

Need most immediate: Fix the stupid window.

Needs 2-9: Watch afternoon television—today it's sports—get his paper, study weekly sales flyers from stores he will not visit to make sure he isn't paying too high a premium to have his food delivered, order groceries, back up the weekly writing time recordings, watch them to make sure there are no irregularities and that the transfer was successful, eat dinner, watching a little more TV or read, depending on how he feels, and get a good night sleep.

The list doesn't help. Allen doesn't want to do a goddamn thing today. But he should. He should make himself. He needs to have a routine.

As soon as the bank card arrives. He can't really do anything before that anyway. He doesn't have any money. Or, he has money but can't access it because his bank card expired yesterday. A new one was to have arrived on Wednesday, then Thursday, then Friday, and when he called an 800 number on the back of his old card they assured him it would be there no later than Saturday or a new, emergency card would be rushed to him.

Not on his porch yet, but at least it's on a delivery truck, scheduled for today, finally. Allen will just have to wait. There is still plenty he could do. Many of the things on his list don't require any money at all. Trying hard to decide if it would be okay to get his paper at least, or maybe back up his work, or maybe he should read a book instead of watch TV today, Allen falls asleep in his chair.

11
WHERE IS THE BANK CARD?

Not where it fucking should be. It's not Allen's fault he's tired. If someone had knocked, he would have heard them. The porch is definitely empty; the package categorized online as DELIVERED at 2:45. It's 4 goddamn 15 now.

Someone stole it while he was sleeping. Obviously. Just like last month when he didn't get to the door right away, and someone ran off with his box with one book inside. That didn't matter, was a minor annoyance. Not having access to his money is a big deal. Allen didn't need his book. He needs that bank card if he's expected to live. This fucking city. It's falling apart. Everyone says so.

Breathe, Allen thinks. Remember to take long deep breaths. All of this is manageable. All he has to do is contact the bank. He doesn't have to call the police. They won't help anyway. Everyone says so.

Banking is handled by phone, and it is a simple process to alert them that his card was not received and should be deactivated. No one needs to freak out. Click a button; card is canceled. But with everything that's happened this week, with how long it took for the card to get here, with the urgency of a broken window and his safety a growing concern, Allen doesn't trust the app. Not totally. He'll have to get on the actual phone and straighten this out. He would not like to handle this through chat. Allen needs someone to hear that he is upset. Thankfully this is easy too. He can be connected with someone as soon as the next person becomes available, a time estimated to be less than five minutes.

"Yes, hello. I'm calling for two reasons. My bank card, my new bank card, was stolen today, and I need to make sure it's deactivated. That's the first thing. The second reason, the more important thing, is I'm calling to find out how quickly I can have a bank card made and what my options are. I'm retired and living at home, and I was promised the card would be sent during the week, when I would be available to receive it. It never got here; it kept getting delayed and when I called on Wednesday they were sure, they promised me that it would be here no later than Friday but it kept getting delayed and now it's gone. I need to have a new one ASAP, and I need you to make this right. I'm in a very precarious situation here, and I need this resolved. Now. Please."

"Of course sir, I'd be happy to help. And can I say that I'm sorry about your stolen card? We'll work to get this resolved as soon as possible. Let's first make sure that the card is turned off and no one has been using it. Where was your card stolen?"

"From my porch. The front porch of my house."

"Okay…thank you…when did you last use the card?" There is no reason for him to sound confused. Allen already explained the situation.

"I never used it. It never got to me. That's what I'm saying. Someone left it on the porch, and I'm sure they didn't knock so it sat out there for who knows how long, and now it's gone."

"All right well the good news is that if the card was never activated it's very unlikely it was used to buy anything, and I'm seeing now that no, this card was never turned on. So that is good news. No fraudulent charges. And I am seeing that you reported the card as stolen through our app…"

"Right. And now I need a new card. Immediately."

"Okay sir, I can have a card sent out as early as Monday…"

"No no no. I've already been through all of this before. I talked to you people on Wednesday, and they were sure the card would be here by now. I can't wait until Monday when another one gets sent out, and I have to sit around my house with no money or anything until it happens to show up. I went through all this last week. This is totally unacceptable. I've been with this bank, totally loyal customer, for over ten years. I want a new bank card made immediately and I need you to guarantee that it will be in my hands."

"Sir, and again I'm so sorry for the loss and for the inconvenience, but since it's a Saturday our options are limited. Is there a purchase you're trying to make? There are some things…"

"There are a lot of purchases I'm trying to make. That's the point. I need the card so that I can go about my life. I don't need a temporary fix; I need my bank card."

"Yes sir. I'm sorry. I understand. In that case your best option, if it's possible, and again I'm very sorry, is to wait until Monday and then visit your local branch. My computer shows that a few of the branches in your area will be able to issue an emergency bank card. You can pick it up yourself there, or I know the branches will sometimes have couriers send out rush orders."

Allen already knows this. He's been through it before the last time his card expired. But last time, his card arrived without incident three days before he needed it. Everything is much worse now. Especially in Baltimore. Can he trust anyone with something so important as the money he spent his life earning, the money he saved and thoroughly budgeted from the time he was 50 until the time he was 80?

No. He will have to leave and pick up the fucking card.

He will have to leave. Which is fine.

That is not a problem. Not like he meant to stay

inside forever. Allen is perfectly capable of doing what everyone else does every day. Unnecessary to completely fall apart because of this. He talks to people all the time. Like when he has to arrange to have the garbage taken from just below his window to the curb or the time he paid someone to assemble a new nightstand. Allen had watched them from the second floor as they carefully carried out his instructions to put the thing together in his back yard and leave it on the back porch. They did a good job, and he left a tip of 25 percent.

"Okay thank you. I will pick up the card as soon as they can make it…I'm sorry I lost my temper. I've…got a lot going on right now."

"I totally understand, sir. I would hate to be in your situation. I'm going to get this started for you, but I do suggest you call the bank first thing Monday morning, tell them your situation, and make sure they have everything they need from you. Anything else I can help you with?"

No that will be all. It's time for dinner. Or it's past time for dinner, but Allen isn't hungry anyway. Instead, exhausted from pacing around the living room, resolving issues of banking, thinking about going outside again, Allen passes out watching an infomercial concerning detoxification and the amount of fecal matter found postmortem impacted in the colon of John Wayne.

12
HOW MANY MORE GODDAMN PEOPLE WILL ALLEN HAVE TO TALK TO?

So many. At least three. Two people at the bank, one person in the car that takes him there, probably. It's all Allen can think about, on this Sunday, when he should be getting ready to go back out into the world for the first time in forever, when he should be resting and making sure to get enough to eat.

Maybe it'll be good for him. Allen could use some new routines like taking a stroll around the neighborhood, but then what if people ask how he's doing, or what he's doing, and what if he has to ask them the same things?

No, a walk will not be a part of Allen's weekly activity when all this is over. The pressure of other people is too much for him.

There are things that could be done but Allen won't do them. There are other ways to pay for online groceries, but he doesn't feel like it. There's enough food to last at least through next week, or the next six months if things get really bad and Allen has to start rationing his reserves.

A single delivery arrives, but it's just his book. Five

years ago, worried that he was getting restless, Allen decided to purchase one book a month. To keep his mind sharp and to keep him busy in the extra time he is of course going to find each day. He likes to look at pictures and accepts the books chosen by algorithm as best suited to his needs. Mostly he receives fancy coffee-table art books.

This one is all fucked up though. The spine is missing, and the red threads that hold the pages together are exposed. It's supposed to be this way, Allen realizes when he is trying to report a problem to the sender. There is a picture of half a house on the front, like a cross-section of a suburban style kind of house, not like the kind you find in Baltimore.

A retrospective of the works of Gordon Matta-Clark. Someone he's never heard of. Who knows why the computer thought he'd care about this more than any other thing? There's a picture of something Allen first assumes is in his city, a half-moon cut from the concrete of a warehouse reading BALTIMORE so that light, new light, hits the floor in a different kind of way. It's not in his city though. Is in New York. Or it used to be in New York. Allen learns online that most of these things are gone, were never around long to begin with. Not a bad book, but there are a lot of words, and the images are mostly of dirty things like old cars and little slices of urban space, alleys. Leftover things, that no one would ever really want to visit.

You need to get ready, Allen tells himself. Tomorrow is a big day. Preparation is essential. Get three solid meals. Figure out what you're doing when you leave, exactly. Take care of your 63-year-old frame.

The most important thing is controlling excitement. Anxiety will help no one. By this time tomorrow this will be over, resolved, and Allen can go back to the business of his life.

He'll have to sleep in the chair again because his bedroom is too hot now, and if someone tried to come in through the trash bag, at least Allen would have a chance to escape through the front door, or he could run upstairs and get out through one of the windows.

Allen does not eat though, not a real meal, just some cheese and crackers and an apple. He doesn't arrange a ride or check the weather but does manage to get in some TV at least.

On Allen's last night inside, after 13 accidental years, he falls asleep watching a public broadcasting documentary about a group of explorers who, while looking for a safe commercial route through the Northwest Passage, got lost, stuck in the ice, ate some of their friends, and died.

BOOK 2

HOW WE GOT HERE

1
WHAT WILL YOU REMEMBER?

Sharon, from human resources, in her blue pantsuit, will remember all the times he was there for her, really saved her ass, and can think of no one more deserving of a peaceful retirement than Allen.

Bill, the shipping and receiving manager who is always wearing the same black collared shirt with black buttons and black trousers, will never forget Allen's constant professionalism, even during the most stressful times. It was a privilege to work so closely.

More attention than he would like; Allen will admit that it is nice. The conference room has been emptied of the long table carved from a single tree, most impressive to new clients, and filled with balloons, compliments, smaller cocktail tables with white tablecloths, and a company-colored blue and gold congratulatory banner.

In two days, he will leave for Baltimore and most likely never see any of these people again. Now is the time to smile and appreciate how lucky he was to have had a job all these years, to have worked for and with each of them. Allen is sure to tell everyone who took the time to attend his retirement party that he is grateful.

Crab cakes and shrimp cocktail catered in honor of

the hometown return. Eileen, in a sweater that is either pink or tan, from accounting, thinks it's funny that they would serve them all a copy of what Allen will be able to get every single day if he wants.

The crab cakes are pretty good though. Allen eats three of them. They're for him after all. For once the extra attention is nice. Beer is served, but Allen only drinks the sparkling wine whenever required by toast. He is toasted twice.

Chocolate cake, assumed to be Allen's favorite because he ordered a slice every Friday from whatever chain restaurant occupied the office building's bottom floor, is wheeled in, cut by Sharon after she is handed a knife, and dispersed through the crowd.

How will he spend his retirement? That's the big question. What everyone wants to know.

Beth, short hair, accounts receivable, read an article recently about journaling, its positive effects on the body and mind, and suggests that Allen cultivate that habit.

Paul, glasses who only worked for the company for six months, has an uncle in St. Michaels, Maryland. Only about an hour away, real up and coming; Allen can slurp raw oysters on a boat.

No thank you, Allen thinks. He hates raw oysters and has been to St. Michaels before. It's too hot and humid in the summer. Impossible to ever be comfortable. Mosquitos are fucking everywhere.

Alice, rides a bike to work every day, an assistant to one of the lead accountants, read an article once about how a young handsome Irish mayor had done a lot to turn the city around by printing signs with bold white print reading BELIEVE.

Andrew, in charge of ordering office supplies so Allen has to talk to him a lot, owns many checked shirts in multiple patterns, thinks Allen should go to a baseball game because Camden Yards is a beautiful stadium, and at night you can see two thirds of the city lit up from the third deck. Andrew might have read the same article as Alice; several new chain restaurants have opened in Harborplace, one of the major tourist destinations. A sign of good things to come.

Mike, market research and kind of a pain in the ass, thinks Allen would like to visit Philadelphia, since that city is in the midst of, and in many ways further along in the urban revival process.

During the second and final toast Dave confesses to knowing Allen best. They've worked together for eight years. The void left by Allen will never be filled. Not in the same way at least. Not if they brought in five guys. Allen really is special. A speech is demanded.

Encircled by his coworkers, next to the nearly eaten cake, Allen thanks everyone for coming, tells the truth when he says he appreciates all the very kind words, and lies when he says he will stay in touch.

2

WHAT WOULD YOU DO WITH ALL THAT TIME?

Sit and think for a second.

"If I knew I had two years to live but I didn't have to work? Something relaxing."

"Where'd you read this?"

"Some article in the waiting room. It was like a medical journal for men, I think. No shit. Most American males die within two years of retirement. Or a significant amount of them do, anyway."

"I can believe it. I really can. When you retire you expire, right?"

"Honestly I'd go crazy without a job."

Allen has a job plus high blood pressure. His doctor just told him. Now he has to ride an overcrowded train back to work even though it's past five, past the time he should be off. He's allowed to have a doctor's appointment goddamnit. It's been scheduled for months. They all knew that.

Boston is frigid. Colder than freezing. Five degrees above zero according to the bank outside his train. Snow from the past three storms sits in mounds on every corner from the doctor's to the office.

He needed the last stop, but the train was too crowded. He couldn't get to the doors in time, so now he'll have to wait for the next one and double back. All these people going home, done with whatever they need to do, while Allen has to go back to work, after hours, to help a total stranger. Some guy he doesn't know who is probably going to be mean to him. Who won't care about what Allen is giving up to be there, will only be thinking about whatever he needs.

Walking Commonwealth toward Downtown, barely noticing where he is going, just the snow blowing in the wind around his ankles, occasionally the advertisements for apartments swept away from wherever they had been posted, muddied by snow and boots. Cheapest prices of the year. Best to rent now. Maybe what he needs is a change of scenery.

Someone lost something. His attention is required. An important business document of some kind. Whatever it is, it's probably gone, but it's important that he displays the proper amount of concern. Show a good effort. This company's reputation being top priority.

Feels like everyone is going the opposite direction as he tries to see how he looks in the mirrored windows of real estate firms, car dealerships, law offices, a high-end grocery store. Impossible though when he's moving so fast, when there's so many people in the way. He cannot see himself fully, is forced to try and piece together what is flashed through tiny cracks in the crowd. Neck in one building. Hair in another. Hasn't caught sight of the pants yet, but they're not his best. It's what happens when you put off doing laundry.

As long as they're not dirty he'll be fine. Fuck it. Allen looks good enough. Stop trying so hard to be perfect. If he can stay calm, show that everything that could have been done was done, it'll all be over soon. According to the doctor, it will also all be over soon if he doesn't learn to settle down. But in a different, more permanent kind of way.

Elevated blood pressure and inflammation. They cause, indicate, many bad things in a human body. He had a hard time comprehending all the information, but maybe blood was getting too big for his veins.

No big deal, the doctor assures. Expected in men Allen's age. Recommends one aspirin a day to keep from clogging. He doesn't need to worry, just make small dietary adjustments, exercise a little more, and Allen will be able to keep working and living a long time. Perform a few simple tasks with regularity. Then he'll be able to be available for whoever wants something from him for years and years and years.

Don't think about that. Just climb the stairs. Look, already getting some exercise. There is a job to do, his job. Allen is a helper. Likes to pitch in. Never gets too emotional about anything.

Seven floors on foot take a toll. Allen must admit he could be in better shape. He's panting when he reaches the top, and that is no way to present himself. Urgency but not panic. Important to show everyone he is in control. It's okay if he needs a few minutes to collect himself and his breath before leaving the stairwell.

Double glass doors unlocked with his wallet, the ID card inside puts out a strong enough frequency so that he doesn't have to take the thing out each and every time he comes or goes.

A coworker is already waiting. Sheila, an assistant from Somerville who loves baseball and her two children, has bangs with layered hair dyed blonde. Her face is pink like it gets when things are stressful at work. "Oh, thank god. There's a guy in the main conference room. He was here yesterday with that big group, remember?"

"Sure. Of course. What did he lose?"

"Ha! You better not say he lost anything. Something he left behind, on purpose, is gone now, and he wants it back. Pretty sure he thinks I threw it away."

"Did you check with anyone who might have cleaned it up?"

"No one here has seen it. The cleaners just showed up. They didn't see it. And they'd know better than to move anything like that anyway. Allen, he's livid, and not being friendly at all."

"What do you think the odds are he took them with him?"

"At least 50 percent. But he wants you to find them. 'Something must be done.' That's all he keeps saying, 'There has to be something you can do. Something has to be done.'"

"So you called me."

"Yeah. Sorry. I really didn't know what else to do."

"You were supposed to call me. I'll see what I can do for him."

"Thanks. Nate's already waiting for me at Kenmore. I was supposed to be there half an hour ago. He's going to be so pissed."

"It's no problem. I've got it. You can clear out for the night."

"Ahh thank you! You're the best, Allen, really. Oh, how was your doctor thing this afternoon?"

"Fine. Nothing exciting."

Gathering her assembled belongings from a beige leather armchair, she smiles, waves, and is gone before Allen has left the reception area.

It's been over twenty years of this shit. At five different businesses.

He liked his second job best, a company that made replacement joints for humans and certain highly specific parts of spaceships, but had been let go when they found a more favorable tax situation in a different state, 400 miles away. Along with a generous financial severance package, he was given a brand-new

George Foreman grill, which he used to make himself a healthier version of the chicken breast and ranch dressing sandwich he ate most days at work.

This current company started as some kind of advertising firm, but now the focus was shifting, content media or media content, which one was still unclear. As office manager it never matters to Allen. He's not part of the decision-making processes. Allen will never be put in charge of any project that really matters to the overall profitability of the firm. It is his job though to make sure things run smoothly for the people who are.

The face Allen finds is half his age (they keep getting younger and younger, the people telling him what to do) and expectant. No smile. No scowl. Simply a person who knows his problem will be solved if he is insistent, if he pushes enough. However he was with Sheila, he won't raise his voice to Allen, not right away. He knows, in the end, one way or another, he'll get results.

The main conference room holds a table carved from one single piece of wood, a whole giant tree. Very expensive, shipped with care from the Pacific Northwest, meant to convey to new clients that no one needs their money. Flip charts from the day's meeting, the one Allen wasn't there for, are still out. Green and red markers on the table. It will be his job to get this cleaned up first thing in the morning, since he missed today.

"Hi sir, sorry. I'm Allen. I was here yesterday."

"I remember. The girl said you would know where my stuff was." Wool peacoat and tan and red scarf are still on, even though it's warm inside, as he leans against the table in a way that indicates he knows how much it's worth but does not care.

"Right, of course. I'm sure we can find them. We're looking for some papers?"

"Not 'some papers.' It was a whole file. And I didn't lose them; I left them here." He doesn't raise his voice, even when he's being a dick.

He's right though. A file *is* different from a bunch of papers. Charles and Chase, having been in business for over 25 years, has an extensive Records Department. It's possible someone from there picked it up, thinking it belonged to them. That would be the best thing right now. An easy fix so Allen can go home and make sense of the information dispensed by the doctor.

"Right, of course. Sorry. What did the file look like again?"

For some reason this is the wrong thing to say, or the wrong way to say it. Allen can tell because the man stands up from the table, and the space between the words spoken gets smaller.

"It was a stack of papers held together by a red butterfly clip. I left it sitting right here, in front of this chair." Not the kind of thing anyone from Records

48

would mistake as their own. "I left it there last night, went to eat, went right back to the hotel, and when I came back today, it was gone. The front page was a plain white sheet of paper, and I need it before I can fly back to Philadelphia in the morning. I've already had to change my flight once. And let me say that if we can't find it, if someone here lost it or threw it out, that's not going to be very good for you."

The fluorescent lights, three lines of buzzing yellow, can give Allen a headache. Especially the center row, its brightness enhanced by the reflection off expensive wood. Tension is starting to build behind his right eye. Think. Where could the papers have gone?

"I'm sorry, how did you say they were bound?"

"With a red butterfly clip. It had seven sections, each with their own paperclip. It wasn't just some stack of papers floating all over the place. They were organized. It was clear they went together; no one should have moved them. That girl already called Records. They don't have them."

"Okay, let me check a few more places. Sorry." Try to speak in a soft kind of voice but still firm, like he's in charge of the situation, without making his headache any worse, without escalating. "But if they're not with Records, and no one else has seen them, it is possible they were thrown away."

"No, I don't want to hear that. I left them here, on

this table, and it's your job to find them for me, isn't it? That was the only hard copy of a very important, and let me say very private, study we paid for. You don't want to have lost this, I promise you."

"Right. Of course. I'm sorry. Let me make a few calls and see if anyone knows anything."

Allen won't call anyone. No one would help him if he did, would politely decline. But if he doesn't get out of this room, and away from this asshole who is treating him like some kind of fucking servant even though he's close to twice the kid's age, Allen is going to totally fucking lose it. He cannot handle this right now. Shouldn't fucking have to. He's got his own problems to deal with. When is there ever time for that?

Allen has no office here, just a cubicle in a mostly empty section of the building. In the corner though, and there are two windows near his seat; plus it's away from where most of the work is done. Alone, the room two-thirds lit, he gets an idea.

To ensure privacy, documents are never thrown out in the regular garbage. The work of disposal is outsourced to a paper shredding company that comes once every two weeks and destroys everything in the back of a big truck, like the kind used for moving small houses. If someone did collect the papers, maybe even Allen, last night when he wasn't paying enough attention to what he was doing and had cleaned them up, they would be in one of the shredding bins, hopefully all together. That's the last place he can check. If they're not there, they're gone.

"Sir, I'm sorry again, and thanks for waiting. There is one place they might be. It shouldn't take too long. If you want to keep waiting here…"

"No, I'll come with you. I need to get this done and get out of here."

The trucks bring machines strong enough to shred a plastic cell phone, so removing paper clips isn't necessary. Allen has a habit of taking things like that out, even though he's been reminded it's unnecessary. The red clip was gone. Each section was in a separate place. It takes more than an hour, with this guy huffing over Allen the entire time, before it's all done, before he calms down, shows any kind of gratitude.

"My man. I will hand it to you, that was impressive. Sorry you had to crawl around so much. Still, if you take better care of your big clients' important papers, it'll save you time. Just a tip from me."

"You're absolutely right, and one more time I am sorry. I'm not sure how they ended up in there."

"Don't worry about it. And hey, if you're ever in Philly, let me buy you lunch."

That won't happen. Allen doesn't even know the guy's name.

The train is less crowded; rush hour has ended. Plenty of seats for him to sit hunched over and stare at the speckled floor of the outward-bound B-line.

All anyone ever does is need things from him. And not in a good way. It's exhausting, draining, and what does he have to show for it? No wife. No kids, thank god, he's terrible with children. An investment property in Baltimore because he could never afford to buy in Boston, no matter how much he saved. That's it. A whole lifetime of working for other people, surrounded by all the things they need, with never enough time for himself.

Those two men, what had they been talking about? Retire and be dead in two years? Wouldn't two years, alone with his thoughts, with the space to live and maybe take one goddamn deep breath without all the asking and people depending on him, with no one clawing for his time and energy, be better than the rest of a lifetime of this? He's 50, unattached. No one is keeping him here. All he does is repeat the same shitty, meaningless tasks every day, in the service of other people.

What might he do? With nothing but time and space, all for Allen?

Didn't he owe it to himself to find out? Hadn't he earned that right?

BOOK 3

THIS CITY BREATHING

1
THE AIR IS THICK AND TASTES WEIRD.

Like sweet, tangy metal. Allen can feel it in his mouth. The outside. That's the point. Stand in front of the open window and take it all in. Prepare. It's been a long time.

He's been squatting for 15 minutes, rising whenever his legs start to feel strained. Bending at the knee, hip, and ankle. Thanks to exercise he can go up and down like this repeatedly. Some men can't and shouldn't feel bad if the movement is impossible for them, his phone's yoga instructor will say. It's not difficult for Allen to put his face to the hole he cut from the window bag because of all the hard work. The strenuous exercise. All the stretching.

Elaborate cakes are made nearby. For a while a TV show about those cakes was, too. Allen would look out and see production trucks and sometimes people loading unusual shapes into vans. The bakery could mold sugar, flower, milk, and eggs into something else and bake it solid. Like a dinosaur or a scene from your favorite movie. Once it was a bucket of steamed blue crabs. Sometimes the scent makes it through the windows, and the house smells like baked goods. Not today though.

No one is loading anything now. It would be nice to have a sense of who was outside, a better idea of what was happening on his street, in his neighborhood, at this time of day. He never needed to know before, and obviously there was no chance to do an accounting of what normally occurs in front of his property on a Monday, in the middle of July, at this time of day. It's completely reasonable to make sure he's as ready, at least in the physical sense, as possible. Allen will take his time, take note of everything he sees now before he starts the exit process. He will not rush outside.

You can't get ready to get ready forever though, Allen tells himself. He knows he's stalling a little; it's understandable, but he must get moving. Probably he's been here too long already.

The car has been scheduled, and that wasn't easy. Not as easy as the app promised. At least they let him link to his checking account, and he didn't need to use the debit card he didn't have. It took longer than Allen would have liked is all.

Rising once more, bathrobe open. The outside humidity wets his stomach, warms his intestines. It's time to get dressed. To put on something appropriate for a trip to the bank. Leave the phone behind. It won't help. Will only distract. Allen spent too much time on his phone yesterday, and it just made him angry. Everything he needs now is upstairs.

There is only one piece of furniture, holding the four items of clothing and a pair of shoes Allen assumed he would wear to his own funeral. A sport coat, dress pants, dress shirt, and necktie. They cost over one thousand dollars all together when he bought them 13 years ago. The suit is a special kind of wool made exclusively inside the homes of villagers on a Scottish archipelago. It is the most expensive thing Allen ever bought for himself or anyone else. Not scratchy, carefully woven and certified by an act of Parliament. The man who sold him the set, who convinced him to spend the extra money, repeated how it was the perfect winter suit for a cold-weather city. Grey and breathable in the right kind of way, the man said. Slimming.

It used to be more so. A little looser than Allen remembers. Probably from all the exercise. There was a time when he would come upstairs to try it on and look at himself in the mirror he hung on the inside of the dresser. It must have been five years since he last saw himself all dressed up though.

Then, like every time, he pictured himself laid out resplendent in the funeral home, the music he chose playing to the most likely empty room, and it made him happy. Like he had accomplished something having this suit and having this thing, this big end of life thing, all planned out. He had thoroughly completed something. The time he was spending inside alone, the time he'd worked so hard for, had been enough. More than enough.

This is different now. He is at the beginning of something and cannot say for sure if he will be successful. His head seems smaller than it should, and the suit is floating around him more than fitting the form of his slender torso.

Is this even an appropriate thing to wear; does it look right on him?

Allen doesn't know. He isn't sure.

What he should be concerned with is how unbearable the Baltimore summer will be for him. Entrance into the world is not advisable according to three different local meteorologists and the people who woke him up on the radio. But Allen doesn't care about any of that. He wants his money, wants to feel safe, and he can't stand another day of being off his routine, with the fucking bag for a window, staring at his phone and his walls and watching whatever on the TV. This has to be handled today, and he can't do it in a bathrobe. He has to go.

Straighten the tie. Make sure the shirt is tucked in properly. It doesn't matter if it would be better to wear just the shirt. There is a sense of wholeness in the suit, of wearing all the things together in the right way. If he starts to sweat a little, the jacket will cover that up. It's a practical decision. It's not just about Allen's personal preferences.

Certain that he looks just right, confident that even the slightly ill-fitting nature of his attire will let the people he is dealing with know that he's gotten in shape recently—they don't have to know how long it took—Allen returns to several messages:

The driver, Jennifer, is arriving in five minutes.

The driver has arrived.

The driver will wait five minutes.

The driver has left.

Allen will be given a poor review, has been charged five dollars. It will be harder in the future for him to get a car possibly.

Jesus Christ one more fucking thing. Why couldn't they have just waited a little longer for him?

There's a lot about this situation Allen doesn't understand. The driver had another fare. It's also company policy to wait no longer than five minutes, so even if Jennifer wanted to wait, wanted to be accommodating, she had no other choice. She did not want to wait. Jennifer is a busy person and has a lot of other things to do today.

Whatever the reason, this is bullshit. It would be totally fucking sensible if Allen just gave up on today, went back to bed, and started fresh in the morning. Justified if he got back in his bathrobe and watched a movie. He's got everything he needs for another day. The bank can wait for him until tomorrow.

But no. This has to be done, and it has to be done now. So much depends upon Allen having access to a working debit card. The map says it will take less than one hour to walk from the door of his house to the door of his bank. How bad can it really be? Allen can handle an hour through Baltimore City in the middle of the day, basically walk right down Charles Street to his money and then have the bank call him a cab or even use his new card to get a different car service application.

The forecast is foreboding, this is true. But Allen will be fine. Ultimately, he will prevail if he is persistent and believes in himself. He doesn't need to worry about water or heat or if he's wearing the right gear.

Baltimore has been worse since the spring according to the things Allen has seen. It's not just the weather that makes this place unsafe. A man was killed by the police in the back of a van. He read three articles and donated $50 to a non-profit the internet agreed was reputable, not overly political. Since then, crime is up. Everyone knows why. Everyone has their own reason why. But this doesn't matter either; it can't matter to him now. Allen worked his whole life so that he could be comfortable. He earned that money, and he needs access to it.

Whatever the city is like now, he will have to endure. He will have to be brave.

No time for ceremony. Allen has to go. This is not a

big deal. It's something he has to do. Turn the handle and walk through both doors, main and screen. Follow the directions. Don't be nervous. Is it really that dangerous? Is the heat really so bad?

2
NOT THE HEAT.

The humidity.

The air packed thick. Dense with moisture. Allen's window bag hole didn't come close to replicating what it was really like outside. He can see the heat, like looking over a smoldering grill. The world wavers. Back and forth. White marble steps could be slippery, but the metal railing feels too hot to touch at first; he grips and then immediately releases before trying again. Not as bad as he thought. Hotter than he expected though. He nearly fell just leaving the house.

Don't get overwhelmed. It's totally understandable, this period of adjustment. It doesn't mean he should give up and go back inside immediately, find another way to pay for the window repair and have the bank send his new card by courier. No, it has to be done this way. Allen isn't a quitter. He is a man capable of taking care of himself.

He can't remember how to go though, and he can't see the directions in the sun, so he has to reascend porch steps to find shade. There are two paths for him to choose from. One that goes entirely over city streets and one that starts with what looks like a short cut through the nearby university.

Probably nicer that way. More green spaces, and it's most likely safer, being a college. A fine way to get started on his journey.

Allen doesn't need a car or practice being outside. He doesn't need familiarity with his surroundings. He needs to believe in himself. To proceed with confidence.

3
THERE IS NO T IN BALTIMORE.

Otherwise he would have taken it. Like in Boston. Always crowded but airconditioned. Even if going from the southwest to the northwest part of the city meant traveling all the way into the center and then back out again, it was a place he could stand still, sometimes sit down. There's nothing like that here, and Allen can't figure out how the buses work. Can't even find the closest stop. Already he's been walking for 40 minutes. It took him that long to get lost and back home again.

It wasn't all his fault. He got mixed up trying to get through Johns Hopkins; none of the signs made any sense or directed him toward anything relevant, and he had to retrace some of his steps. Whatever short cut he thought he saw on his phone must have been wrong. Probably the map needs an update.

In the middle of the university, surrounding a statue of a guy on a horse, there was a student protest. What Allen assumed were students since it's a campus. Megaphoning Black Lives Matter. Signs reading Justice For Freddie Gray. He didn't want to bother them, and at that point he had given up hope of actually making it through the campus to Charles Street on the other side, so he decided the best thing to do was go back the way he came.

But it's all very sad. Allen remembers how upset he felt reading the news, in the spring. He would like to do more. He should give more money, he thinks.

Another thing that's impossible without a card. Allen needs to focus and get this done.

A lot of work to be back where he started, outside his own house, where he should give up for the day, go inside and rest.

He is no quitter though. Never has been. Allen must keep walking. Determined, but not moving so well. The space outside heavy with water weighs Allen down. It's a lot harder to breathe this dense air than he remembered.

Sometimes in his dreams he has to run someplace, but he can't run fast enough. His legs don't work right. He lacks the strength to properly lift them. It's a common phenomenon, easily interpreted if researched online. He feels like that now, like all his energy is being used and he is not getting the results he wants, the typical results a man could normally expect from this level of exertion. He's fighting against the suit. Skinny, fit, Allen's body is pushing forward, but the Harris Tweed is saying no.

Sometimes also in his dreams he will have a hard time operating the buttons on his phone. He'll be trying to order something or call someone, and he can't press the right things until in his dreams he screams out in frustration. Too bad when he checks his phone this time everything easily works, even in the sun, with his fingers smearing sweat on the screen whenever he touches the glass. Allen would rather be dreaming. He can confirm at least that he's finally going in the right direction.

Or he will be. Allen needs a break. Just a second to sit on his marble steps which he hoped would cool him off some but aren't themselves and lean his head against the house, stare at the hole left behind by the missing streetlamp.

Scratchy, like compressed sand against the back of his skull. The formstone is rubbing off; flecks of fake brick sprinkle down his neck, rest under the collar of his shirt. This isn't helping, Allen thinks, it's only making things worse, and it's ridiculous to have covered up real brick with something approximate. He researched this. Extensively a long time ago, and would have liked for his own house, the one he will die in, to be made of only the original exterior. But those renovations are expensive, and because in many instances the installation of the formstone was done improperly, removing it does permanent damage to the integrity of the rowhouse. Easily his least favorite feature of the house, something only seen in Baltimore, it was fashionable for a time to make the outside of a place look different from the one next door. He didn't care much when he bought it since he planned on renting it out, and he didn't care much when he moved in, once he learned how much it would cost to fix, since he had no plans to ever see the outside. Allen hates the way it feels now though.

There is still a long way to go before arriving at the bank. He shouldn't think about that. Better to keep moving. If all that counted was distance travelled then yes, this is going poorly, but that's not the only measurement that matters. Doesn't Allen deserve some credit for overcoming an initial, reasonable mistake, for not totally freaking out and giving up and going home when that would have been a completely justified response?

He'll take the credit, even if he hasn't earned it, even though the smart thing to do would have been to go back inside his own house and at least get a drink of water and a little bit of food. Allen has water bottles inside that he could carry with him, remembered again before he left but worried they would look unprofessional and would clash with his very nice suit.

This sense of accomplishment is all he needs to forget he's already too hot and a little dehydrated. He pushes himself up, onward.

The Paper Moon Diner is close to where he lives, to where he's standing now, after walking for over a half an hour. But it's proof he's on track, the landmark he noted when he reconsulted the map, once he realized he was lost.

If he had any money he'd walk in and order something. He knows he would. Like it was no big deal. Like he didn't by accident stay inside forever, like he was just some regular guy. Actually that seems really nice. Allen is getting very thirsty.

Oppressive, this heat. That fucking car could have waited. He wasn't upstairs too long, wouldn't have complained about paying whatever extra they wanted to charge him as long as he got the ride and didn't have to drag himself through the middle of the city in the middle of the summer, overdressed in the elements and sweating more fluid than he has to spare.

Check the phone again. Check to make sure it still works and that he has to walk.

It still works; he can still press all the buttons, the imaginary buttons since his current phone is a flat sheet of glass. A little harder to operate, but not because he's dreaming—because his hands are too sweaty. First, he'll try to dry his thumb and pointer finger by rubbing them together. When that doesn't work, he'll wipe them against the lining of his jacket sleeve and in his pants pocket. Still each time he leaves a wider perspiration smudge on the screen.

According to the Internet, he can find a hack,

a taxicab with no license, but he has to stand on the corner and hold his arm a certain way, not down, not up, he doesn't get exactly what he's supposed to do, so it's probably a bad idea and, right, he can't pay for the cab anyway. He'd have to have some kind of awkward conversation in which he tries to explain his situation and the driver gets very angry with him and drives off in a way that makes his tires squeal once it becomes clear that something is needed but can't be paid for.

No buses, no car services, no trains except one red line that is of no help to his cause, but it doesn't matter. He refuses to live another day inside without being able to freely spend money. That's his right after a lifetime of work and saving and sacrifice. He's earned it. He'd be over halfway there if his goddamn phone had an actual updated map, like you'd think it would, because what's the point of having all that technology if you're going to get just as lost as he used to get whenever he had to go someplace new.

He's made it out of Hampden, his neighborhood, for the first time in 13 years, past the painted screens and real red brick, burgundy cut with tan, past the pink formstone and the second-floor bay windows.

An argument might be made that things couldn't be going any better. He walked through a college campus. Saw a bunch of people gathered for a good cause. Kept his shit together when he most needed to. Sat outside on his steps for a second. Walked past a diner.

True, a lot has gone wrong already, but Allen isn't going to dwell on things he can't change. Just keep walking south, he'll be there soon, inside the bank and then back inside his house and if he needs to stop then that's okay too, there has to be a place he can slip inside to ask for directions or maybe even some water if he has to get out of this heat.

4
YOU CAN SIT
FOR AS LONG AS YOU NEED.

"It's totally cool." The person working the counter treats him kindly. They have mushroom earrings. Allen would like to be cool, but he is the opposite. Can feel the sweat dripping from his armpits and rolling down his back. May he please have some water.

Yes, for sure. It's self-service. As much as he likes.

Legs already cramping, heart beating too fast, and still a long way to go, this seemed like a good place to stop. The next road he had to cross was four lanes with a median, all the grass burnt brown by the same sun attacking him, what he needed to escape from. Any farther without a break was going to be too much. Been over an hour already. The whole trip shouldn't have taken this long.

Allen looks around at the visual detail of the interior of Red Emma's Bookstore. He remembered ordering from here once during a day devoted to small business shopping. A photographic history of Baltimore, then and now, with pictures of how the city looked at one point next to how it looked when the book was printed. He could have bought it cheaper from a bigger online site, but that wasn't what mattered then. It felt nice to do something good for something small.

Finally, thankfully, Allen made a right decision. He barely had to explain his situation: under normal circumstances he'd be able to pay, has actually purchased online from this establishment, lives in the neighborhood, kind of, but his bank card, etc. The employee just waved their hand, smiled, made eye contact, pointed to the water. Allen was invited to stay until he is ready to go again.

Nice in here, pleasant and calm, even with all the talking. Allen always liked coffee shops and houses. Before he was transferred to the Boston office, there was a place to go sometimes on the east side of town for vegetarian brunch on the weekends, a three-floor rowhouse with a piano anyone could use, boardgames, and couches called Funk's. He wasn't a vegetarian, but it was close to his house, and there was a lot of space to sit and relax, random people would come by and play music, using the instruments already there or bringing their own, and they always had carrot cake, his favorite.

This reminds Allen of that.

Even though it looks different, it laid out different, that was the kind of place that would be nice to a person who came in off the street looking for water, even if they weren't wearing an expensive suit, even if they were acting a little strange.

Below a poster for something called Future Islands is a tray full of pebbled plastic glasses and a long clear tank of water. Allen drinks three full cups without regard for how it might look before sitting down at a table as far away as possible from the front windows facing West North Avenue, from the bright and hurtful summer. The entire back of the space sells things to read. Racks of probably homemade magazines. An assortment of hard and soft covers. Behind a separate register, directly across from the one selling coffee and food, someone is looking at a copy of *The Passion According To G.H.*

Allen has never heard of that book.

"Can I get you something to eat? You don't have to pay. We have a couple muffins and a scone from yesterday. They're still really good. I love our muffins. They're banana walnut. The scone is blueberry, I think." It's the mushroom person, pink hair short in the front and long in the back, a mullet sort of, in black boots with yellow stitching and one-piece blue coveralls, like a painter, substantiated by sporadic splotches of paint on the legs and arms.

"No, thank you. I appreciate that though. Really, I'm okay. Just a little hotter than I expected." The first exchange Allen has had with a human face in 13 years. Not bad so far. He doesn't count when he first came in, when he asked for water, since he was a little too discombobulated from the heat and the extra walking to pay close attention to what was happening. It will all be okay as long as he can rest for a minute. Even if this mushroom person probably thinks he's homeless.

"Right? I'm from Vermont, and up there we winter in, you know, but I swear down here it's like a summer in kind of situation. Find a pool or some other water to jump in; go see some dumb movie just so you can sit in a theatre. We even went to the mall once just to get out of the heat... Well, rest as long as you want. You sure you don't need anything?"

"No, I am okay, but thank you." Make sure to pronounce all the words right. Allen must really look like shit for them to come over and check on him, to offer something free to eat. But at least it's an approachable kind of shit. At least he's not freaking people out. They didn't seem concerned about his clothing; they're not *that* wrong a thing to wear. He wouldn't be allowed to stay if he were acting too weird, right? Maybe he's doing okay.

After another glass he's ready to leave, thinks he is, but should have one more. Just in case. Sit and drink it slowly. Don't get a stomach cramp.

A man close to his own height, about his own build, but with much darker hair and white skin that had clearly seen more sun than his own, enters carrying a leather briefcase. Shoulders back, chest out, he walks to the drink counter, smiles the whole time he orders.

Then claims two tables, pushes them together, nods at Allen who is now an empty table away, before he leans back and looks at important things on his phone.

It's a nicer suit than this burial wool, he can tell. A lighter kind of cotton, and it fits him better. A newer cut with the skinny lapels Allen sees well-dressed people wearing on TV and online. A modern suit for a modern man.

If he hadn't moved the tables, Allen would still know he was waiting for someone. He worked with people like this all the time before. He's early on purpose and after another minute is joined by a Black man in a similar jacket, light blue instead of gray, t-shirt, jeans, and brown leather dress shoes. They shake hands; the second man notices the first has a drink, goes to get his own.

"Hey, Dan, thanks for meeting me here."

"Sure, nice place. I've never been here before."

"We should have some office space of our own by next month."

"That'll be an upgrade. No more meetings in coffee shops for Mike soon! We'll have you on your way!"

"That's what I'm hoping for. How's your boy?"

"Doing really great, actually." The leather briefcase, oily looking when it gets closer, slams onto the extra chair, and from it Dan produces two papers, one with words and one with circles in different colors.

"What year is he now?" Mike takes from his canvas shoulder bag a black moleskin notebook, halfway used, and a pen with an extra fat grip while he examines the papers Dan presents.

"It should be his second coming up, but something tells me he's not going back." Dan doesn't change the tone of his voice. he's told this story before probably, will tell it again in the next meeting. Allen never felt that kind of confident. The control in his voice, the way he's able to keep his timbre constant while pulling out papers and displaying them all over the table where he is sitting and the empty table he brought over so they could have the space they needed.

"Everything okay?"

"Yeah, everything's great. He started a little business in his dorm room freshman year, and it took off. Said he didn't see the point of paying over 120k for school when he could be making money on his own now. Since I was the one paying, I didn't disagree."

"Takes after his dad. I love it. What's the business?"

"He buys and sells shoes."

"Money in that, for sure."

"There's money in everything if you do it right. He cleared sixty grand in his first eight months."

"That's not bad. Not bad at all. Sneakers?"

"Sure, sneakers mostly. He designed a computer program that can make purchases from different websites all over the world simultaneously so when these things come out, and some of them are extremely limited, he can buy multiple pairs while most people are waiting out in the rain in front of some store in Brooklyn or wherever. We went to visit him last spring, and his room was floor to ceiling in boxes of one kind of shoe. You know the one? From the rapper?"

"I've seen them. Pretty weird looking if you ask me. But it's a brave new world, I guess."

"Sure, it's new, but really, when you drill down a little, it's no different from anything else. Supply and demand. Do what you can to get control of the supply, especially when the demand is already there. The shoe companies and computers do most of the work for him. He doesn't have to worry about production or marketing, doesn't have to handle supply chains or any of those headaches, just has to have some idea of what's going to sell, and he says that mostly has to do with how limited a sneaker is. Then the kids and collectors go crazy and will pay ten times over retail for a shoe that probably cost five dollars to make. I'm proud of him. And let's be honest, whatever gets him out of the house fastest, right?"

"Lot of money in a rapper's shoe, I guess."

"Lot of money in exclusivity, which, moving right along, about this license, we've got a guy from Oregon and a guy from Colorado coming in…With the people I know in the state legislature, I think you've got a real chance to win one of the 15, which is going to, right off the bat, be worth five to ten million, even before you really get started, before you've put a seed in the ground…"

Allen has an exclusive kind of life. Needs to get back to it. The bank won't be open forever. And the sooner this is over, the sooner he can get home, to that existence curated only for him, that he made, that he earned.

Hard to leave a place with free water though. In this heat. If not for the detour, the totally understandable mistake, he'd be almost done by now. Would be inside a bank that's a little too cold, maybe offered a bottled water or even a coffee, which he would turn down. Just the water would be fine.

Allen is smart for stopping, but even with the hydration, the respect he was given, the time to rest, he is wearing out. This is the last chance to turn around safely and go home, but he won't.

He has to keep going.

Will not accept defeat.

Determination. Focus. Stick-to-itiveness. He has these qualities. It's how he got this far.

As long as he keeps his jacket on, no one can see how much sweat he's already lost.

5
NOT A BRANCH
JUST A MACHINE IN A WALL.

Stupid goddamn phone. This isn't where he's supposed to be. An ATM, not the actual bank, brick and mortar. He knew it, should have trusted his gut and not the directions. All the banks are in one place in this town, the big banks, the major branches. They are all in a place not here. In front of a strip club. Covered in stickers, but at least the screen works thank fucking god. How much more is going to go wrong today? This week? How much can Allen be expected to overcome?

"Hello there sir. Looking for some entertainment this afternoon?"

"No thank you, just need to use the ATM."

"Well there you go, most secure ATM in Baltimore. Got its own bodyguard." Points with his thumb to the bigger man standing between them, the one who opens the doors.

We're Sorry; This Card Is Expired. Please Contact Customer Service Or Visit Your Nearest Branch For Assistance. No shit. Allen knows. What do you think he's doing here? Stupid goddamn bank machine. He needs to think for a second. The phone isn't to be trusted anymore. Allen has been disappointed too many times. After going the wrong way, having to get free water from a coffee shop, already running late, it's possible he's not even close to where he needs to be. Allen might be totally fucked.

He's either going to have to find the place himself or ask someone for directions. All untrustworthy options. Who would he even ask?

"Ready for the season?"

"You know it. Hello there; looking for a little lunchtime fun?"

"Think they might do it this year?"

"Nope."

"Come on, where's your faith?"

"At church on Sundays. Nope, I think they're going to suck. I think fucking Pittsburgh is probably going to win it all. My fucking father-in-law is never going to shut up about it. Hey there, friend, welcome, welcome." Finally, a man who is probably a banker, he probably came right from the place Allen needs to be because of how he's dressed in a dark blue suit with a bold tie and brown Chelsea boots, walks into the door opened, gives a two-finger salute to show appreciation. "Nice to see you again. God I fucking hate them."

No one in Baltimore likes anyone from Pittsburgh. It didn't used to be this way, but when the football team relocated from Cleveland they left behind their name and history and brought with them a rivalry born out of proximity and like-mindedness. Everyone embraced the new enemy quickly. Whenever he had to go there for work, his family would say things like, "Oh no so sorry better be careful. Ha ha ha."

The last time, on a trip to Burgettstown, Pennsylvania, he and four other people stopped at an all-you-can-eat Kentucky Fried Chicken. Billboards advertising the chance to eat all a person wanted in 20, 10, 5 miles. They stopped mostly out of curiosity. Some of the thighs were oddly shaped, and the legs had too much breading, but nothing was inedible. They were simply the pieces that weren't quite good enough for the regular, full-priced meals. Everyone was helpful, and when they went out for drinks in Pittsburgh proper on their last night, it was all charming, according to one of the people on the trip, he doesn't remember who, and he agreed.

But Pittsburgh sucks and so does everyone in it, apparently. Because their team is named after the steel industry, the mills that signified the hard-working, blue-collar nature of its fans, and his team is named after a poem. People in Boston felt the same way about the people from New York, and one time when he went to Oregon for a hiking trip, someone at a gas station asked where he was from and then said, "Hey, as long as it's not California!"

Goddamnit. Focus.

Stop listening to those people and figure out how to survive. He should have been inside a long time ago.

It's lunchtime and crowded even though no one should be outside who isn't supposed to be, who doesn't absolutely have to be. Allen has to be. It's essential for him, but how important could it really be for all of them?

Streets packed with people and shit air and water, he's fading, head getting lighter from the sweat and exertion, having a difficult time getting enough oxygen, the right kind, no matter how hard he tries he can't get enough in his lungs.

No one can survive in this, he's got to find the place he's supposed to be, it's the only way. The only way he can go back to how things were—not great, kind of boring, but comfortable, and he always had space and always could breathe okay. That's all he ever needed. Allen isn't greedy. Just a little space to be left alone and take as many deep breaths as he wants and not have to listen to anyone or anything unless he decides it's what he wants.

So far from that now, literally and the other way. It's a mile back to his house. He can't walk that. He couldn't walk this even if he didn't get lost. Maybe he could make it back to the bookstore, but what good would that do?

If he can get to the bank, he'll get a card and

some cash, and he's a customer there, plus it's all the goddamn bank's fault anyway, they couldn't get him his fucking card on time, the one goddamn job they had that mattered, so when he gets there he's going to make sure he's treated right, the manager is already expecting him, and he'll tell them they need to update their fucking address on the phone too, however that works, because it's totally fucking unacceptable that in this age something like that would be inaccurate. It's not at all possible Allen made a mistake. He checked several times.

The phone is not to be relied on, but he must be close. All the banks are packed into this area. Always have been. They change names but not buildings. It has to be one of these. Everyone is moving on this street except the door guy and bouncer. They're always in the same place. It would be a good idea to ask them, but he won't.

Allen would rather do it on his own.

That's the best way. It has to be. Impossible that he is that far away from his intended destination. He's not that bad at executing a simple task. Going back the way he came worked once before. Retrace the last leg, back to where he knew he shouldn't have turned left even though the phone said so. He has to be able to find one bank at least, right? If he could just find one, even the wrong one, someone inside surely could tell him where and how to find his bank, and it would be airconditioned and they'd have a water cooler with pointed paper cups that he could put to the skin starting to peel away from his lips. Could take away the filth forming in the corners of his mouth and cool him to the core. Allen's overheated, overworked core.

"Busy today."

"It's the AC."

"Doing anything this weekend?"

"Wife's family is coming in; we got passes to the aquarium."

"Not bad. Haven't been there in a minute. Nice to have the passes. From the wife?"

"Yeah, one of the few perks of that job. Not sure we could take the whole family otherwise. But my daughter loves that stuff. Says she's going to be a marine biologist and study cuttlefish."

"What's a cuttlefish?"

"It's like a squid. They change shape and color and shit. Pretty crazy." They twist together into a sliver of shade from the overhead marquee to view his phone screen.

"Whoa, that is crazy."

"They're smart too. That's what she says."

"That's cool. They got cuttlefish at the aquarium?"

"Nope."

"You sure?"

"Yup. She asks every time."

"Too bad. Indoor rainforest is cool though."

"Most definitely."

What are the symptoms of heat exhaustion? Or is this heatstroke? What's the difference? In the beginning Allen thought a lot about the ways he might die. It made sense that it would be on his mind, so he tried to prepare. He never found the study that confirmed what he heard on the train that day, so he had no other information. Didn't know what to expect, and even though he'd like to imagine drifting off in his sleep, life slowly slipping away while he, peaceful and content, smiles at his ceiling fan, it was more practical to imagine situations less serene. Slipping and falling and slowly bleeding out in his bathroom or choking on a piece of food, a heart attack was probably painful but over quickly, or maybe it would be something long and drawn out like the cancer that killed his father.

Never had it occurred to him to prepare for this kind of discomfort. The oversized suit is even bigger now. He must have lost weight on the walk. The dress shirt is attached to his skin like shrink wrap, the necktie is too tight, he can barely swallow—not that there is anything to gulp down, not even a tiny drop of spit to wet the inside of his mouth. Dry and hot and there is water all around him but Allen can't drink the humidity.

He won't make it. Not to any bank, not up the street even; he can't go any farther.

"Hey man, everything okay? You need some help?" That came from behind, didn't sound friendly, must be another person waiting to use the machine. Standing here too long, unsure what to do, Allen takes the expired, rejected old card protruding from the slot and sways, left then right, then takes a few steps toward the strip club men.

"I'm sorry, can you help me? I'm…looking for…my bank…"

He hears himself say the words, feels his head hit the kneecap of the bigger gentleman, who, because he is a bouncer at a strip club, is used to old white men passing out on him.

6
ALLEN IS CONNECTED TO NOTHING.

Thank god. In the movies, TV shows, when you commit a crime and pass out, sometimes you wake up handcuffed to the bedframe. At a certain level the transgression will require someone to watch outside the door—two layers of security, human and inanimate. Even then the person being observed will often escape easily, offscreen. Allen isn't chained to anything, so probably no one is waiting outside the door to ask him any questions.

Weird thing to think first. He needs to spend less time watching shows. Allen knows he did nothing wrong.

Also, oh good, he is not dead.

And he *is* connected to something. Two things.

Allen has proof he is alive. They hooked him up to a machine that says so, a heart monitor, and he's connected to a pouch of fluid through a tube running out of his arm. Makes a fist and feels the needle. It's IV fluid, whatever that is made of. He is being replenished. The sun is out. It's still daytime. He's in a hospital.

"Well good morning, nice to see you awake." A nurse has entered, speaking quickly and not looking at him. All Allen can see is dark brown hair pulled tight into a ponytail.

"Is it morning?"

"Sure is."

"Monday?"

"It's Tuesday, hon. All day."

Tuesday means he's been here all night. His house was empty all night. Anyone could have come in, could be there now. Great that he didn't die, but of course he never made it to the bank, that's the last thing he remembers, that the place he needed to go wasn't where it was supposed to be, he got overwhelmed and was pretty sure it was all over, felt like he was going to drown on dry land. Did he hit his head on some guy's knee?

"What happened to me?"

"You passed out from exhaustion. You shouldn't have been out in all of this. You're lucky to be breathing today."

"Well...yeah...I'm sorry...but I didn't have much choice. I mean, how did I get here."

"A car dropped you off."

"I didn't come in an ambulance?"

"No, they said out front it was just a car. But look, whoever did it saved you a lot of money. Those ambulance trips cost a fortune."

"How long have I been sleeping?"

"You've been out for about 18 hours now. You wore

yourself out, that's for sure. Get some more rest, and I'll come back and see how you're doing in a little while, after I finish looking in on everyone else."

"When can I go home?"

"I'm going to have to check with the doctor about that. They make those calls. Might want to keep you for observation. Let's get the rest of those fluids in you at least, and if nothing seems too out of sorts, then you can probably be on your way. Where's home?"

"I live in a house. A rowhouse. In Hampden."

"Oh I'm from Hampden. I mean I was born there. We left years ago though." Now that she knows they are from the same place, Allen is a little more interesting. She's short and white and maybe 40. Green scrubs.

"What were you doing out in all this?"

"It's complicated. My window, my bedroom window was broken and..."

"How awful! I'm so sorry! Broken how?"

"It was an accident. The light in front of my house was stolen." No one was personally attacking Allen.

"That's just sad. They'll steal anything that isn't nailed down these days, and I guess even if it is. Nailed down I mean. It breaks my heart what's happened to this city."

Allen would rather not have this conversation, but does he really have a choice? Could he just get up and rip this stuff out of his arm and walk out in his hospital gown into the city, recovered and triumphant? That doesn't seem like something he's capable of.

"It never used to be like this. You used to know your neighbors. Now half the city's on god knows what, and it's the grandparents raising all the kids. It's too bad. It was such a nice place."

Think now. Try to remember. Because he never made it to the bank, his house was open, actually physically open all night. Empty. He never even turned the porch light on. If someone got in last night, would the neighbors on either side have heard? Would they have called the police? Will there be cops waiting for him when he gets home? Allen hopes so; if his place was broken into, he'd like the police to handle it.

"Between you and me, that's why we left. No way my husband was going to send our kids to a city school. I mean, I went there and it was fine but it's not anymore. We moved out to Cecil County…It must have been 20 years at least. It's quiet, and we have our own yard for the kids to play in. We just got a dog. The kids love it."

The first thing to do is go back home. Get out of here and go back home. Then he can restart the process again. Learn from the mistakes to avoid failure the next time. He has to get this done. Is determined to be successful.

"But you know what the best part is? I drive west in the morning and east at night, so on my way to work and my way home, I never have to drive with the sun in my eyes."

"Right, yeah, I had cousins who lived in Bel Air. They used to say the same thing. And I'm sorry, I really do need to get out of here and back home. Do you think you could check on that for me? As soon as possible, I mean. I know you're busy. I just don't want to leave my house open any longer. Oh, and I don't think I can pay for a car."

"Don't worry, hon. I'll call you a car. I've got a great customer rating too, so let me check with the doctor, and we can get you out of here ASAP."

"You don't have to do that, really. I mean I can pay, I just need to get to the bank, and…"

"I told you, don't worry about it. Us Hampden folks have to look out for each other, don't we? We're not going to put you out on the street. We're not like that here, no matter what anyone says."

They do sometimes put people out on the street, in their hospital gowns, all alone. Allen saw. It became such a big story that it was on broadcasts outside of Baltimore. He will not be one of those people though, thankfully.

"Okay, here I go. Just rest and maybe watch some TV…Ooh I love this show. Best episode too."

In a corner, attached to a metal arm bolted to the ceiling, a program is running without sound. It doesn't matter. Allen has seen it before. It's a comedy with romance, and in this episode the main lady tells the man who she will eventually marry that she loves him. He can't say it back though. Physically he cannot pronounce the words, just makes a bunch of L sounds before saying something like "I…l…l…left the pasta boiling on the stove" or whatever and runs away.

So fucking stupid. It happens on a lot of shows. Allen hates it. Can't believe it's a part of the real world. What kind of person couldn't say three words? The other one always gets their feelings hurt, always suffers from their partner's inability to speak.

He has, in his adult life, told two different people he loved them. He's not sure if he meant it either time. It was said to him first. Allen thought it would be too uncomfortable to say nothing back but did have some sense of the harm caused by withholding as well. He cared about them that much at least, that he didn't want them hurt. Allen, for whom many things are difficult, found it easy to blurt out what he needed to say. It didn't mean anything in the end. Both relationships dissolved in a normal, adult kind of way and everyone moved on. He can never understand why it isn't repeated to make the other person feel better. Why go to the extra effort to make someone sad?

"Good news, hon, you're free to go whenever you're feeling up for it. Let me know when you're ready, and I'll get that car for you. Just make sure you get plenty of rest and fluids, okay? We don't want to see you back here anytime soon. Next time you might not be so lucky."

Now he has to go home and start over, do this all again tomorrow, if he doesn't return to a house thoroughly plundered. If he doesn't have a new set of problems to deal with.

This wasn't luck. It was a total waste. Of an entire day.

7
EVERYTHING IS EASIER
WHEN YOUR SHIT IS ALL TOGETHER.

Even better when you've had some practice. Allen's got it this time. He knows he won't fuck it up.

What happened was nothing to be ashamed of. He had no choice but to leave the way he did. Could have happened to anyone, getting lost, passing out, spending the night in the hospital. Allen is brave for trying.

The house was fine. No sign anyone even noticed he was gone. A little past three on a Tuesday when he walked back through the front door. At his discharge the doctor was very clear that he was to take extra care of himself over the next week. More rest. More good food. Lots and lots of water. Keep an eye on his breathing. Let them know if it becomes difficult.

One week has passed, nearly. The window was replaced, new clothes were ordered, all without a functional card. Turns out there are a lot of ways to pay for things now.

Today his objectives are clear, two-fold: get to the bank (he doesn't want to live with that failure) and then reimburse the person who put him in a car and sent him to the hospital, saving his life and money by avoiding an expensive ambulance trip.

It's the least he can do. Nice to think that someone did a thing for him, made something easier, even if they didn't need to, and Allen believes in repaying what he owes.

What Allen cannot do is walk again. Fortunately, there are multiple car applications. Only one thinks of him as irresponsible. He gets to start fresh with a new rating. It's a better service anyway. The reviews agree. To make sure he is not late, Allen waits on the front porch. Five minutes early.

There are trees on his street. A big selling point, not something you're going to find in every neighborhood in Baltimore, the realtor said. Some of them have wooden boxes built around the base with flowers inside. One is decorated with hearts tied to branches with the words Black Lives Matter and Rest In Power Freddie in thick handwritten letters. Probably a child made them. One of the ones Allen can hear yelling sometimes.

Shattered window gone, but on the sidewalk where the streetlamp was removed, the hole remains.

Almost as soon as his door shuts, the neighbor, the grocery cart woman, opens hers. Allen figured she might. It's probably something of a big deal that he is outside; he's not totally oblivious to that. He can't wait inside though and risk missing the car, and he talked to a whole bunch of people the last time, so he can handle this.

"Is everything okay?"

He's only seen her from the peephole in his door. Up close she's a little older than he is, or maybe she's had a rough life.

"Yes."

She starts to go back inside but pauses, looks at all of Allen.

"Are you sure?"

"Yes, I have to go to the bank." There's no point in explaining any further. It's the truth.

"Oh. Okay. So long as you're all right. Do you know when they're going to fix the lamp?"

"I'm sorry. I don't."

"When I called, they told me next week. I said, 'I wished you'd do it faster.' It's a safety issue, after all."

"Well, thank you for calling."

"You're not going to the store too, are you?"

"No, just the bank."

"I forgot to get milk today. If you stop by a store, will you get me one of the half gallons of milk? Whole milk. Just a half gallon. If I get more than that at time it goes bad."

"Yes. But I'm probably not. I'm sorry."

He will not, absolutely. Allen isn't trying to make any new friends and certainly doesn't want to be responsible for anyone else's whole milk.

Right on time a gray minivan pulls up to the curb.

A tinted window slides down.

"Hi, you Allen?"

"Yes, thank you for the ride." To his neighbor: "And thanks for the info about the light. Sorry about the milk."

Much better this way, even if he has to talk with the driver, who's wearing a black hat with the numbers 1966 on the back. An old oriole on the front. Headed south again, just like last week but safer. Without having to feel Baltimore so intense and pressing and overbearing, Allen can see it. He likes the surfaces of his city. The pastel rowhouses, rippling concrete, and bay windows hanging out from second stories.

"Sorry about this traffic. I swear it keeps getting worse."

"It's fine. I'm in no rush today."

"Hey, good for you. Day off?"

"No, not really. I have a lot to do, actually. I just gave myself enough time to do it."

"That's the secret." With the palm of his hand, the driver presses the horn, holds it down for at least three seconds. "Sorry. Almost got hit just there."

On the horizon a gothic cathedral and a metal sculpture of a man and a woman farther down the high rises of the Inner Harbor, where Allen used to work before they sent him to Boston—go or lose your job, essentially, so he went. Left his home.

That's what Baltimore was, but it doesn't feel like home now. Just where he lives. The rowhouse feels like home. But that's all he ever wanted. The space to breathe and be left alone. Nothing complicated. Was that asking for too much?

Focused only on the task most important to him, Allen saw very little last time and still failed. He's grateful now for the chance to take it all in from the comfort of a rideshare with working AC. A nice little getaway from his regular existence. He should call a car more often, even if he never has any place to go.

"These fucking lights." The driver tried to whisper, but Allen heard. They made eye contact in the mirror. "Sorry. We've just hit every light on this street. My least favorite part about driving in the city. None of the lights are synced up so you just fucking inch along."

Allen nods. He understands. At least can pretend like he does. "I'm fine. But sorry you've got to drive in it. I do appreciate the ride." He's still going to be 45 minutes early, by his own calculations.

"All they need is a computer program. My brother told me. Like it's this totally simple thing they could do and we'd all be moving much faster. Plus it's worse today because they're doing something to the monument."

"Oh." Brick rowhouses line both sides of the street, brake lights on the cars in front. When the minivan crests a hill, Allen sees the line of red stretch out, toward the water, the harbor.

"You know they say that's the first statue ever made of George Washington in this country. Before the one in DC even."

"Yes, I heard that."

"You know what else someone told me? That isn't even George's face up there. I had a guy in the car the other day...what did he say he was...he worked at one of the Army bases out in one of the counties and was a professor at night I think...whatever, it doesn't matter... he told me that the guy who carved the statue wanted more money, or didn't get the money he was supposed to get, and so he put his own face onto the monument. But I don't know. I didn't find anything like that when I looked it up. Good story though."

"That is a good story. I never heard it. But I believe it."

"Yeah, people will get all kinds of mad when the money isn't right. Welp, here ya go. Hope you enjoy the rest of your day."

"Yes, they will. And thanks and good luck with those lights."

Allen gives a 15 percent tip. No, twenty. He can afford it.

8
NOW IS THE TIME.

"Don't listen to what anyone else says. Property is dirt cheap in Baltimore right now."

It's a different consultant from last Monday at the coffee shop, but they talk the same. This one is skinnier, pale. Probably early 30s. The price paid for arriving early. Listening to the things people say in the lobby of a bank at 15 minutes till noon.

"I really don't think you're right here."

"Too cheap to pass up. I'm telling you."

"How many did you buy?"

"Ten so far. Four on the east side by Hopkins, four over by the Poe homes, two near Druid Hill Park."

"By the mall?"

"Close by, yeah."

"How are they, like what's the condition?

"All vacants. Mostly totally empty. Only one of them even has any pipes left."

"What are you going to do with them?"

"Nothing. Sit on them until it makes sense to do something."

That's what Allen is doing. Sitting until it makes sense. Being ahead of schedule means he gets to take it easy today. On his porch. In the car. Now this leather chair, surrounded by glass cubes with bankers inside and a giant safe with a door the size of the whole room, floor to ceiling, with the giant handle that looks like a ship's steering wheel. Good to know that even if he can't get to his money, they're keeping it safe.

"Make a decision on the kids yet?"

"The head is still pushing pretty hard, laying it on thick, telling me about the new endowment funds, the things they've done to make the sports teams better, all this stuff. Calls me once a week. But that's where you send your kids if you want them to be painters or journalists or to, like, make films or something. It's not necessarily where you send them if you want them to be doctors or lawyers, run a business."

Allen went to a Baltimore private school. But he didn't become a doctor or lawyer or any kind of artist. Still, he did okay for himself.

"What are you going to do?"

"See who makes the best offer. Where'd you go to school again?"

"Hello, Mr. Wentworth? Thanks for waiting. We've got you all set up. Just follow me." The bank manager, just like he asked for, smiles down at Allen. A thin Black middle-aged woman in a purple suit.

"Thank you."

"Are you having an okay day?"

"I am."

"I like your shoes."

"Thank you." Allen likes them too. His feet feel much better today.

She leads him to one of the workspaces that line the edge of the bank lobby, a little bigger than all the rest, reserved for the manager. It says so on the door. Inside is simple, nearly empty except for a cherry wood desk, official-looking though out of place in this world of clear, square rooms. Only a laptop and two photos, both facing her chair, but Allen can see in the reflection behind her that one is a wedding photo, she got married on a beach and her husband was barefoot, and the other is of her among a group of similarly aged women holding a banner with Greek letters.

"You wouldn't think 90 degrees would feel so nice, but it does."

"It really was brutal last week."

"We missed you on Monday. Hope you stayed out of the heat!"

"Yes, sorry…The day got away from me I suppose."

"That will happen. Well, here you go. So sorry you had to come all the way down here for this. We've had some problems with the mail lately."

"It's fine, really." What good would complaining do?

"Anything else I can help you with?"

"Yes, actually. Can you help me withdraw one hundred dollars, in two fifty-dollar bills?"

Ninety degrees feels nearly pleasant. The bank lady was right. Allen could walk around in this for hours if he had too, he bets. Next stop is near by, though. The place where he fell, was saved. Actually he hadn't missed the bank by that much, was close the whole time, just like he thought. Doesn't even need to consult a map. He knows where he is.

Same street even, a few blocks past a parking garage and a couple of convenient stores with signs in the windows, advertisements losing color from the constant sun, but what's inside is inaccessible behind roll-down gates.

At an intersection with a traffic cop in the center, Allen can see the marquee from before, the one he passed out under, and two men by the door again, though one looks a little smaller than he thought. In his left and right pockets are the two bills, folded three times so they fit easily into the palm of his hand. You don't want to be flashing cash all over the streets.

Closer though, and he's almost sure one of them is the wrong person. The big guy is definitely smaller today, the one working the door and shouting is the same.

In his mind, in his house before leaving, it all went

smoothly. He gave each of them a fifty-dollar bill, slid it to them with a handshake, real subtle, thanked them for their care the other day, walked away upright and proud. Now he has to think of something else. Street is empty, thankfully.

"Twenty-one girls inside, You looking for..."

"Hi, sorry, I was here the other day."

"Shit, man, I remember. Nice to see you back on your feet so soon. Thought for sure you died on the way to the hospital."

"Yes, I know, and thank you. It was all just a...I didn't mean to be any trouble."

"Honestly, happens all the time."

"Well, I did want to thank you." Allen thrusts his hand into his left pocket, gets the bill, realizes this is the wrong shaking hand, extends it anyway.

"Oh, okay thanks." It's less awkward once the money has been exchanged. "You want to come inside? We got 'lunch specials.'"

"No, thank you. The other gentleman, the one who was with you last Monday. Is he here?"

"No, sorry. Not today."

"Do you know when he works next?"

"Can't say that I do. You just want to give him some money? You can give it to me; I'll make sure he gets it."

"No, thanks. I would like to give it to him myself."

"I know he works at a bar in Fells, on the water. On the corner. Might check there."

Always more to do than Allen thinks, always more complicated than he imagines. Just one more task, though, right? Then he can be done with all this and get back to keeping to himself and doing his own thing.

9
THAT'S THE GUY.

Allen thinks. He's pretty sure. Ninety percent.

Here the streets are cobblestone. Put down hundreds of year ago, when Baltimore first started to grow. Strawberry gelato drips pink, a single tear, onto Allen's new boot. Wiped away before it can leave any kind of mark. Five dollars for a small, but why not treat himself. After all he's been through this week. Sharing the bench is a broken pen, yellow and pink neon.

It's been a long time. Since last week and since Allen has been to this part of the city, what he used to tell people was his favorite neighborhood. Would have retired here if it made economic sense, but it cost too much to be so close to the water and the nightlife.

Eat slowly. In appreciation. It's also a good way to spy on the doorman working the corner bar and restaurant. That is almost definitely him. Still a good idea to go slow. Be sure. Rushing into things has not worked out well in the past.

The heat has broken. People are out with their families getting lemonade and shellfish, taking pictures by the water. There's a man holding a sign: "Why lie? I need a beer." Fortunate to even get a bench; the couple who came in behind him and their kid are consuming whatever they got leaning against the Pitango wall. When he's finished, Allen drops the cup into a trashcan with a sticker reading Eat Bertha's Mussels and Follow Us on Social.

Definitely that's the guy. Soon Allen can go home and rest, at peace, not feeling like a total failure or like he owes anyone anything.

Money is in the right hand, in his pocket. The timing is a little off though. Allen arrives at the same time as a couple who intend to go inside, are probably guests or regulars at least since they are greeted with a "welcome back."

Allen will have to improvise.

"Hi, I'm sorry, you probably don't remember me." Only an inch taller than Allen but at least fifty pounds heavier, he looks at Allen's head, feet, everything in between. Twice.

"Oh right, hey buddy. Nice to see you standing."

"Yeah, right, I know. That why I'm here actually." He doesn't want to make anyone nervous, but something is a little wrong, Allen can tell. He's making him uncomfortable but doesn't know why.

"Okay…and?"

"I just wanted to say thanks and repay you."

"Oh, ha. I thought you were going to be one of those guys who tries to sue you when you help them or something. Had me scared there for a minute."

"Ha, no. I'm not one of those guys. Just wanted to pay you back."

"No need, just doing my job." He waves away the hand extended, holding the three-times-folded fifty dollars.

"But please let me give you this."

"You really don't have to. Not like I'm going to let you die in the street in front of me."

"Really, it's the least I can do. You probably did save my life. And…the nurse…she said you saved me money by putting me in a cab…"

"Wasn't a cab, was just a car. The club pays for them. They don't want people passing out all over the street in the middle of the day. You picked a fine place to lose it, actually. Probably the best place in the city to pass out."

"Oh…I mean okay…but still…it would make me… I'd just be a lot happier if I could give you this." The money is out now, clearly visible, his arm fully stretched.

"Okay. I'm not going to argue with you too much. But you don't have, like, PayPal or anything?"

"No…I mean I should…I can get it if that's better for you. I have some other apps…"

"Look, it's fine. I mean, if you insist."

"Yes, thank you. Please." The bill is transferred, hand to breast pocket, and for the first time in a week, Allen inhales fully.

He did it.

"Coming inside? Nice in there."

"No, I have to get back."

"Right then. Be careful out there."

Before calling the car, going back to the comfort that has always been his most important priority, Allen sits down by the pier, sees the markings of new shoes reflected in the water. Tries to think of what color that is, the harbor, but can't come up with an accurate description. He's never been good at that sort of thing. Not blue, not clear, opaque. Like the bag once stretched over his window.

Spent most of a life here, his life, in Baltimore and the area around. And they were wrong about this place. It wasn't so bad. A beautiful city breathing, red brick and pink formstone, pastel row houses descending streets lined with trees still growing. Allen had seen all these things while out walking, and many people had been nice to him.

But this isn't for Allen anymore. Baltimore is not his home, hasn't been for a long time. Just a container for his house. That's all he ever wanted: time and space for himself. He doesn't need anything more than comfort.

EPILOGUE:
BACK INSIDE WHERE HE BELONGS.

Allen knew he could do it. Feeling safe, accomplished, he has to admit it wasn't such a bad adventure. The break in routine might have even been good for him. Got several free cups of water and a checkup from the hospital, which wasn't free, but he might as well use the insurance he's been paying for all these years sometime, right? Met a lot of new people, was able to solve a difficult problem on his own, mostly.

Allen won't be undertaking anything like this again though. He missed his house and his routine. Most of all, missed his writing time and his comfy chair. No need for all that excitement, though he will try to be more mindful of his screen time. Stop falling asleep in front of the television. You need to make adjustments. Every now and then. Like when he gave up all social media a few years ago because it was obviously making him depressed.

Besides, there are more interesting things than social media. On Allen's first day inside for the rest of his life, he found an article online about earthquakes and how humans haven't kept records long enough in places like Portland and Seattle to know that eventually the earth will shake so hard that it liquifies for a moment. Allen learned about the phenomenon before, from a public broadcasting documentary.

It's called liquefaction. Sometimes it happened to the ground under prehistoric animals. They sink fast, and then, when the earth reforms, find themselves stuck. Unable to move, they slowly starve to death, surrounded by other unlucky creatures who happen to be there at the same time. It must be a horrible way to die, but it's perfect for studying the kinds of species that don't exist anymore.

ACKNOWLEDGMENTS

This City Breathing came into existence over a period of 13 years, the result of the support and conversations from and with some of the following people and works of art.

Mos Def and Talib Kweli are Black Star—Where the title of this book comes from, and whose work helped me understand that if one of us isn't free, we are all to blame.

Goddard College, for teaching me how to explore, trust, and read more than I wanted to.

Donnelle McGee, for unwavering support and encouragement to write the book as I saw it, and for being more patient than I probably deserved.

The amazing team at Thera Books, Colleen Mills, Jenna Sumpter, Carla Baja, Nia McGee, and Mona Z. Kraculdy for all the work they did in bringing this tiny, weird book into the world and for letting me be a part of their journey.

Douglas A. Martin, for always working harder to understand the writer I wanted to be, doing what he could to help me get there, and telling me first you need to see the room, then the person in the room.

Bhanu Kapil, for being a super cool destroyer of language and teaching me that Post-Colonial Literature is everything that came after colonialism.

Rafael Alvarez, one of the first writers to help me see that Baltimore was beautiful, that being from there is something to be proud of, and for career advice that one time.

The Lauder-Deans, for support emotional and financial, and for keeping me connected to the things that are most special. I love you.

ABOUT THE AUTHOR

Chad Dean is a fiction writer, propaganda publisher, and cofounder of Splimm and Weekend Review Kit, two digital platforms dedicated to mainstreaming cannabis and ending the racist drug war. Chad has also written articles on these topics for a variety of online and print publications and has worked in business development and marketing for the emerging cannabis industry. Chad's fiction explores related themes, examining the way privilege operates in our society and questioning the role of white male voices to shape our dialogue and culture around literature.

A graduate of University of Hartford, Chad earned his MFA from Goddard College. As a white Chad, he spent hours and days flaneuring the streets of Baltimore with his then young daughter. He currently lives with his family in Portland, Oregon and stays mostly for the city's superior coffee, cannabis, and communist leanings. *This City Breathing* is his first published book.